The Dragon
Who Couldn't
Help Breathing Fire

Denis Bond
Illustrated by Valeria Petrone

Hippo

Other titles by Denis Bond and illustrated by Valeria Petrone

The Train Who Was Frightened of the Dark
The Granny Who Wasn't Like Other Grannies
The Monster Who Couldn't Scare Anyone

Scholastic Children's Books,
Scholastic Publications Ltd,
7-9 Pratt Street, London NW1 OAE, UK

Scholastic Inc.,
555 Broadway, New York, NY 10012-3999, USA

Scholastic Canada Ltd,
123 Newkirk Road, Richmond Hill,
Ontario, Canada L4C 3G5

Ashton Scholastic Pty Ltd,
PO Box 579, Gosford, New South Wales,
Australia

Ashton Scholastic Ltd,
Private Bag 92801, Penrose, Auckland,
New Zealand

First published by Scholastic Publications Ltd, 1990
This edition published 1994

Text copyright © Denis Bond, 1990
Illustrations copyright © Valeria Petrone, 1990

ISBN: 0 590 55738 6

In a small cave on the side of a
mountain, lived a dragon.
Nobody ever came to visit him.
He didn't have any friends at all.

Even the milkman refused to go near the cave. He always left the milk at the bottom of the path. Like everyone else from the village, the milkman was afraid of dragons.

One day the dragon decided to disguise himself. He put on some trousers and an old jacket. He stuck on a false moustache and placed a flat cap on his head.

"Nobody will know I'm a dragon now," he said as he set off towards the village. "But I must remember not to laugh." When the dragon laughed, he always breathed fire.

The dragon strolled along the river bank, where a man was fishing. "Come and join me if you like," said the man. "I've got a spare fishing rod."

All morning the dragon and the man sat, fishing. They chatted like old friends. The dragon felt so happy. Suddenly there was a tug on the man's fishing line.

Together they hauled their catch
from the river, but it was nothing
more than an old boot.
"What a silly looking fish," laughed
the man.

But the dragon laughed too and a
sheet of flame shot from his mouth.
The man was terrified. He dropped
his fishing rod.
"You're . . . you're a dragon!" he
stammered.

The man ran away, shouting,
"A dragon! Help!"
A tear rolled down the dragon's face.
"But I wouldn't harm a fly," he said
to himself.

The dragon dried his tears and
caught the next bus into the village.
The bus was full and a little boy
offered the dragon his seat.

The dragon sat behind a woman
who bounced her baby up and down
on her lap. The baby was pulling
funny faces and the dragon tried,
very hard, not to laugh.

But he just couldn't help it!
His laughter shot flames across
the heads of the passengers, sending
them all screaming from the bus.
The bus skidded to a halt.

The sad dragon walked the rest of
the way to the village. As he passed
shops selling all kinds of food, he
began to feel very hungry.

Arriving at a tea-shop, he peered through the window and saw people tucking into sandwiches and cakes. The dragon's tummy was rumbling, but he had no money to buy food.

The waitress saw his nose pressed up against the glass. "Poor man," she said. "He looks so hungry." She waved at him, but the dragon thought she was shooing him away.

As he was about to leave, the waitress rushed out of the tea-shop and grabbed the dragon's arm.

"Come and sit down," she said. "I'll get you something to eat."

The waitress picked out a big cream cake for the dragon's tea. But as she brought it to the table, she tripped over a little old lady's handbag.

The waitress tumbled to the floor,
and when the customers saw her face,
all covered with thick, gooey cream,
they laughed and laughed. She looked
so funny.
The waitress laughed too.

The dragon tried hard not to laugh, but he just couldn't help it. Giant flames leapt towards the counter, where they burnt all the cakes and toasted all the sandwiches.

"I'm sorry," said the dragon, when
he saw what had happened.
But no-one was listening. Everyone
ran, screaming, from the tea-shop.
"It's a dragon! It's a dragon!
Help! Help!"

The tearful dragon decided to go home. He knew he'd never find a friend, because he just couldn't help breathing fire.
On the way to his cave, he passed a small cottage.

"Hello!" he heard a voice call, and a little old woman hurried from the cottage towards him. "Don't come too near," he warned her, kindly. "I'm a dragon. I breathe fire!"

"I don't care if you're a monster from outer-space," said the little old woman, "just so long as you can help me."
And she pulled the dragon through her cottage door.

"My stove has gone out," explained the little old woman, "and I can't cook my dinner."
"I can light it for you," said the dragon. "But you'll have to make me laugh!"

The little old woman popped a saucepan on her head and danced a very funny dance around the kitchen. But it wasn't funny enough to make the dragon laugh.

She cart-wheeled across the room,
singing silly songs and pulling
silly faces.
But still she couldn't make the
dragon laugh.

Then she had an idea. She grabbed
her feather duster and tickled under
the dragon's arm.
The dragon roared with laughter.
He was very ticklish.

With the flames that shot from
his mouth, the dragon lit the old
woman's stove.
"Would you like to stay for dinner?"
she asked. "There's plenty here for
two."

The dinner was delicious, and both
the dragon and the little old woman
had plenty to talk about.
"Will you come and see me again
tomorrow?" asked the little old woman.

A very happy dragon climbed into
bed that night.
"I've found a friend," he chuckled.
And as he did so, a tiny flame oozed
from the corner of his mouth.